BABAR'S
MYSTERY

LAURENT DE BRUNHOFF

SCHOLASTIC INC.

New York Toronto London Auckland Sydney

ISBN 0-590-30963-3

12 11 10 9 8 7 6 5   5 6 7 8 9/8 0/9

People come from all over the world to Celesteville-on-the-Sea. It has the most beautiful beach in the land of the elephants. King Babar and Celeste are vacationing at the Grand Hotel with their

children—Pom, Flora and Alexander. They are strolling on the promenade that runs along the shore. "Wait for us," Arthur and the Old Lady shout from the terrace.

The sun is very strong, so big umbrellas line the beach. Some bathers play, some relax, and others go in the water. Babar and Celeste are happy. The Old Lady, however, finds that there are too many people. "I adore this place, but there is too much noise," she says with a sigh. "I need quiet and solitude to write my book. I can't work at the hotel."

"But it's very simple," Celeste tells her. "You can work in the lighthouse. There you will hear nothing but the splash of waves and the cries of gulls." The Old Lady is delighted by the idea and she settles in at once with her cat, her typewriter and a stack of paper. Babar and Celeste go along with her on their bicycles. Arthur arrives ahead of them—on his motor bike.

When they return to the hotel, Babar, Celeste and Arthur are greeted by shouts from the children. "The piano has been stolen! . . . Some furniture movers came to get it. They said they were going to bring another one for the concert. But they left in a truck and have not come back! Nobody guessed that they were thieves!"

Flora proudly shows everybody the glove she found on the sidewalk. "If we can just find the owner of the other glove, we will have the thief!"

"A valuable clue," cries Arthur. "I will start an investigation at once."

The Old Lady does not plan to come back to the hotel for lunch. Instead, she is going to remain at the lighthouse until evening. So Babar and Celeste go to the market to buy food for her picnic lunch—some fruit, bread and ham, as well as some cookies.

Arthur, meanwhile, is questioning a glove merchant. "Madame, have you recently sold a pair of gloves like this one? It is the glove of a thief, we think."

"No, young man. I don't sell this brand. But I think that my friend Patamousse at Mont Saint Georges has some like it. Go see him. He will be glad to help you."

The Old Lady has asked that
absolutely no one bother her
while she is writing her memoirs.
So Babar sends the lunch up
in a basket by using a rope
and pulley.

Arthur appears on his motor
bike to tell the results of his
inquiry.

"Well, well," Babar decides.
"We will all go to Mont Saint
Georges."

Babar drives the whole family in his shiny red car. Arthur, of course, prefers to go on his motor bike. Mont Saint Georges is only a few miles away. It looks very imposing behind its thick fortresslike walls.

"You know," says Alexander, "at high tide Mont Saint Georges is surrounded by water—just like an island. And then you have to take a boat to get there."

Babar parks the car and walks toward the castle ramparts with Celeste, Pom, Flora and Alexander. Arthur makes sure that his motor bike is standing securely. . . . What a crowd! The tourists are coming to Mont Saint Georges in busloads.

"Our friend the Old Lady was wise not to come with us," says Celeste with a laugh. "She would have detested all the hubbub."

"But it is so beautiful," says Babar, "that we must not forget to take back some post cards for her."

The narrow streets are full of sight-seers. Babar, Celeste and the children stroll about, looking at all the souvenir and antique shops. Finally Arthur locates the shop of Patamousse the glove merchant. "Sir, have you sold a pair of gloves like this?" he asks the hippopotamus.

Unfortunately, the merchant has sold many such gloves so he cannot give Arthur any very precise information. "But," he says, "I seem to recall that the last customer to buy a pair like that was a lion."

"Ah," says Arthur, "perhaps he is my thief."

Pom, Flora and Alexander are tired of walking, so the whole family
sits down at an outdoor café to eat some delicious crêpes, a specialty of
the region. Arthur seems thoughtful. He has noticed a huge rhinoceros
at a neighboring table. "That is a strange-looking fellow," he whispers.
"Do you think he might be one of the thieves?"

Celeste tells him not to suspect people just because of the way they
look. "You must have other, better clues," says Babar. "It is difficult to
be a detective."

At last it is time to leave and all of them walk away from the castle
ramparts only to find that their car has disappeared! "Where is my car?"
cries Babar. "Someone has stolen my brand-new car." Babar is in a state.
He goes around asking all the bus drivers if they have seen his red car.

One of them remembers
seeing such a car driven
by a crocodile.

"No, you are wrong,"
says another. "It was a
lion."

A third driver claims to
have seen an elephant at
the wheel.

"Which one am I to
believe?" Babar wonders
helplessly. "Come, we will
have to go back by bus."

Back at the hotel Babar gathers his family around and tells them: "In a little while a new statue is going to be unveiled at the Celesteville Seashore Theater, and I must give a speech. A big crowd will be there. I want you to keep your eyes open."

Right away Pom, Flora and Alexander go off to the theater.

Outside it, the decorators are hanging up beautiful garlands of flowers in the town square. One of them, a lion, walks past with a box under his arm. On his left hand he's wearing a glove—just like the one Flora found!

Is *he* the thief?

Pom, Flora and Alexander rush off to tell Arthur the news. "The lion who is decorating the square must be the one who lost the glove! . . . So he must also be the one who stole the piano! . . . And the car, too, perhaps!" Quickly they return to the square with Arthur, who stands in the doorway to observe from a distance. But now the lion, high on a ladder, has put on his other glove. So, *he* cannot be the thief.

Later on, Babar is finishing his speech in front of the statue, which is covered with a sheet. Arthur watches the crowd of spectators, hoping that some new clue will put him on the trail of the thieves. Finally Babar says, "And I wish much joy to all the future audiences at the Celesteville Seashore Grand Theater." Then, raising his trunk, he prepares to uncover the statue. Everyone holds his breath. At last they will see the famous gold statue!

Babar gives a sharp tug at the sheet, the cloth slides off. . . . NO STATUE! . . . Someone has stolen it! In its place there is a crude dummy made from a barrel and some pieces of wood. . . . "Catch those thieves! Go get those thieves!" shouts the crowd. "There must be a whole gang of them." "First the piano, then Babar's car, and now the statue!" "This is just too much. We have got to catch the scoundrels."

Arthur jumps on his motor bike and drives it onto the main road. As he turns the corner, he spies a red car speeding away . . . Babar's car! On the back seat there is an enormous, peculiar-looking bundle.

"That thing pointing up into the air must be the statue's trunk," says Arthur. "I have found the thieves at last! I will not let them get away this time." Though he tries hard, he cannot see the driver's head.

Where have they gone?
Arthur has lost the trail
at a street corner.

Since he is on the road
to the lighthouse, he stops
to see the Old Lady.

He wants to ask her
if she has heard a car
go past.

"You are looking for a
thief in Babar's car?"
exclaims the Old Lady.

"Yes, I did hear a car just now. It must have stopped very near here."

But what is going on in that little shed? They hear laughter, then a piano.

Arthur sneaks up quietly and puts a large box under the window.

He climbs up on the box and peeks in the shed. . . . What does he see?

Four crocodiles are dancing with joy around the unwrapped statue, which shines with a golden light. Babar's car is there, and the piano, too! One of the thieves, the one who is wearing a glove, cries out with a sneer: "Ha! Ha! Ha! I would have liked to have seen Babar's face when he discovered the barrel and the pieces of wood!"

"Hurry up," says another. "We must not be late to our meeting at the harbor."

Arthur has learned enough. He quickly slips away because he wants to get to the harbor ahead of the crocodiles.

From his hiding place, Arthur sees the crocodiles on board a boat with a rhinoceros whom he recognizes at once. It is the one who was eating ice cream at Mont Saint Georges!

"Good work, my friends," the rhinoceros is saying. "Here in this briefcase is half of the money I promised you. You will get the rest when you deliver the loot at my place on the other side of the bay. Keep the piano for your hideout since it amuses you to play with four hands." Arthur rows away quietly in his little boat, and a little later he goes to warn Babar. Together, they prepare a plan.

Night has fallen. The crocodiles have already loaded most of the loot on a big boat. They think they have been very clever. They don't suspect that Arthur and Babar are watching them from a hiding place behind the lighthouse.

Suddenly, at a signal from Babar, the Old Lady, who is on watch at the top of the lighthouse, begins to shout, "Stop, thieves!" The crocodiles stop in their tracks, flabbergasted. "There is somebody up there," shouts their leader. "Ah, but it is only the Old Lady!"

"Ah-ha! Old Lady!" shout the crocodiles. "Have you come to watch the sun set? ... Well, be quiet. No one can hear you. Ha! Ha! We will take you away with us on the boat. You are not going to have a chance to tell Babar about our business." Having shouted those words, the four crocodiles, who are not very smart, rush into the lighthouse after the Old Lady.

What foolish fellows! That is exactly what Babar is waiting for. The minute they are in the lighthouse, he slams the door. Without a moment's hesitation, the Old Lady gets into the empty basket. Immediately Arthur lowers her to the ground and pulls the rope down. Now the crocodiles are prisoners! Arthur rushes off to get help, while the four thieves moan about their bad luck.

The next day everyone on the beach is reading the newspaper account of the exciting event!

ROBBERS CAUGHT!

Discovered by Arthur and the Old Lady, the robbers—a gang of four crocodiles—have been arrested thanks to King Babar's bold strategy. The courage of our dear Old Lady has won everyone's admiration. The leader of the gang, a rhinoceros, intended to sell the statue and leave on a trip in Babar's car. The Coast Guard caught him while he was trying to escape. As for the theft of the piano, it seems to have been the idea of the four crocodiles, who call themselves musicians. . . .

SCHOLASTIC INC.